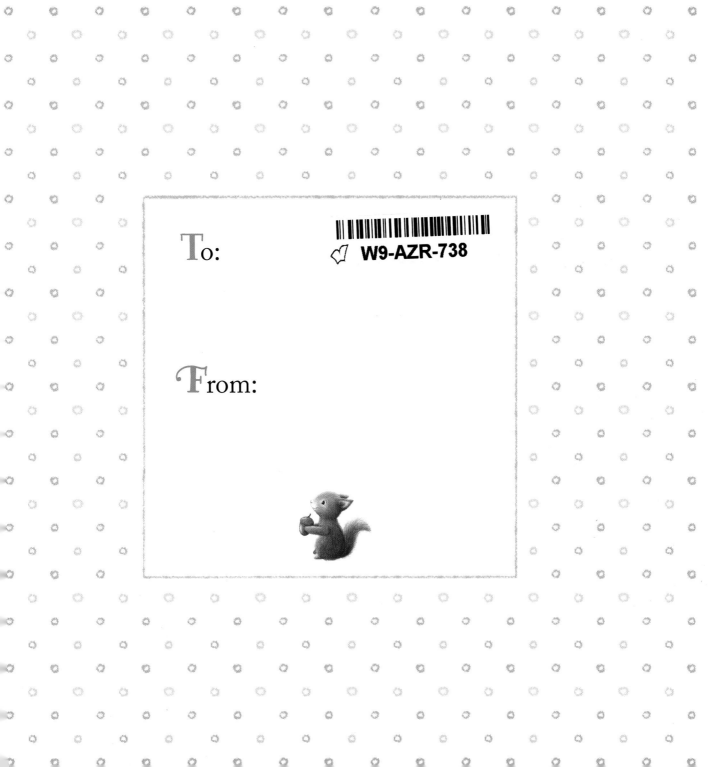

To:

W9-AZR-738

From:

Why a Son Needs a Dad

by Gregory E. Lang   pictures by Gail Yerrill

Adapted for picture book by Susanna Leonard Hill

sourcebooks
wonderland

From the moment that I saw your beautiful face,

held you close to my heart in a father's embrace,

I promised to help you grow with strength and grace.

My dear one, my sweet son, my boy.

Sunshine and laughter, mischief and fun,

trouble and tenderness rolled into one.

I'm grateful each moment that you are my son,

love yourself as I love you, dear boy.

I'll show you that life's more than work and routine.

You have to find room for yourself in between.

Take the stage, play guitar, write, or grow something green.

Find passions that you love to do.

When you're filled with questions and wondering why

the earth slowly spins or how stars fill the sky,

we'll search for the answers together and try

to discover and explore something new.

When challenges come and put you to the test,

don't be afraid to step up with the rest.

If you're not number one, you've still given your best.

It's trying, not winning, that counts.

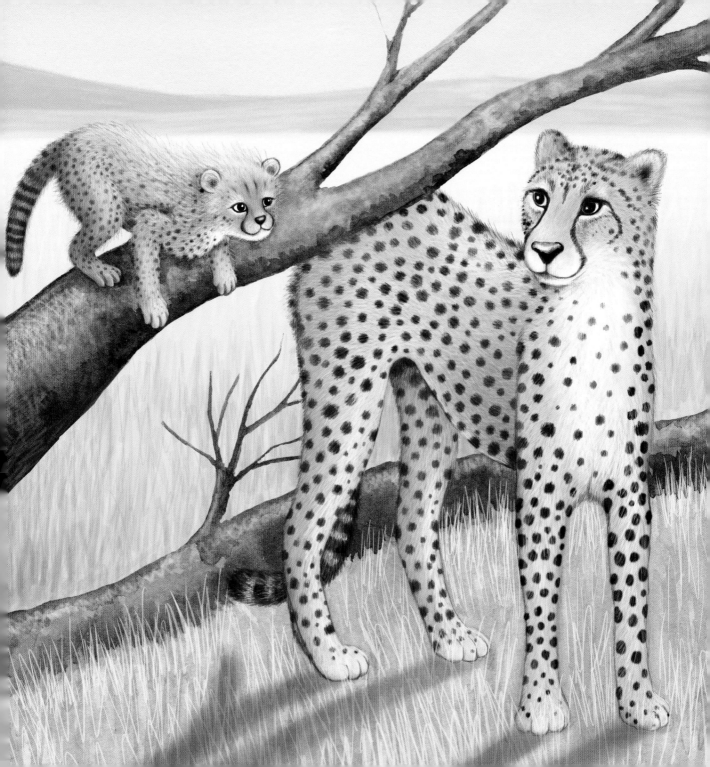

You can follow my footsteps, but sometimes you'll need

to think for yourself, make a choice, take the lead.

Independence and confidence help you succeed.

Be the light that shows others the way.

When *see-for-yourself* leads you where it led me,

to sunburn and bug bites and poison ivy,

we'll grin at each other because we both can see,

the greatest adventures are wild.

If it rains on the day of your costume parade,

or your school trip's postponed, or your team is outplayed,

when life hands you lemons, make sweet lemonade.

Chin up 'til next time, my boy.

I know that friendship is fun, games, and cheer,

but also means being a listening ear.

When friends need support, let them know you are here.

Be the friend I know you can be.

If you're angry, confused, disappointed, or sad,

need to let your tears fall in the arms of your dad,

I'll put you at ease, no matter how bad.

You must feel what you feel, precious boy.

Embrace all the people and places you see,

the wide range of languages, interests, beliefs.

Though people may differ from you and from me,

there's a whole, rich, wide world to explore!

Be as nice when you win as you are in defeat.

Always be fair. It's not worth it to cheat.

Be proud and upstanding, humble and sweet.

In all that you do, play your best.

Remember to honor the people you know,

to be kind and respectful wherever you go.

Conduct yourself well as you blossom and grow,

and you'll earn respect in return.

I'll teach you to love who you are, dearest son,

to dream your own dreams, be inspired, have fun.

Make mistakes and remember you've only just begun.

Imagine, discover, and be YOU!

From the boy that you are to the man you will be,

I love who you are and the promise I see.

You make me the father I dreamed I could be.

My dear one, my sweet son, my joy.

To Dad, with love and great appreciation. —GEL

With love for my boys and their dad, and for my brothers, who are all amazing dads. —SLH

For my mum and mum- and dad-in-law, you're all amazing!
And to my Abigail and William—Love you always xox —GY

Why a Son Needs a Dad copyright © 2004, 2021 by Gregory E. Lang and Janet Lankford-Moran
Text adapted for picture book by Susanna Leonard Hill
Illustrations by Gail Yerrill
Cover and internal illustrations copyright © 2021 by Sourcebooks
Cover and internal design copyright © 2021 by Sourcebooks

Sourcebooks and the colophon are registered trademarks of Sourcebooks.

All book illustrations have been painted with watercolor and then details added in Photoshop with a Wacom Intuos tablet.

Published by Sourcebooks Wonderland, an imprint of Sourcebooks Kids
P.O. Box 4410, Naperville, Illinois 60567-4410
(630) 961-3900
sourcebookskids.com

Library of Congress Cataloging-in-Publication Data is on file with the publisher.

Source of Production: Jostens, Inc., Clarksville, Tennessee, USA
Date of Production: December 2021
Run Number: 5024707
Printed and bound in the United States of America.
JOS 10 9 8 7 6 5